Annie  and the
ALIENS

Annie and the ALIENS

EMILY SMITH

ILLUSTRATED BY PAUL PARKS

Andersen Press • London

For Charlotte (E.S.)
To Aud, the world's greatest Mum (P.P.)

First published in 2001 by
Andersen Press Limited
20 Vauxhall Bridge Road, London SW1V 2SA

British Library Cataloguing in Publication Data
available
ISBN 0 86264 695 2

Phototypeset by Intype London Ltd
Printed and bound in Great Britain by
Mackays of Chatham Ltd., Chatham, Kent

Chapter One

KEEP OUT

Secrets can be fun.

But what if someone keeps a secret from you?

That isn't such fun.

In fact it's not fun at all.

As Annie Brown found out . . .

The best thing to do when someone keeps a secret from you is to pretend not to care.

The worst thing to do is to hammer on their bedroom door, and shout.

Annie hammered on James's door and shouted, 'Let me in!'

They were in there. She just knew.

James, Will and Arthur.

James was Annie's elder brother. Will was her younger brother. And Arthur Vance was James's friend, who was staying.

They had disappeared right after lunch. One minute the kitchen was full of boys. The next minute it was empty. And James's door (when Annie went up to have a look) was tight shut. What's more, when she turned the handle and pushed, it wouldn't open.

Hah! She knew at once it was a plot. An anti-Annie plot. Maybe even an anti-*girl* plot.

'Let me in!' she cried

Silence.

'Let me in or you'll be sorry!'

Silence.

Annie thought. Then she made her voice all honey-sweet. 'There's something I need to tell you. Could you let me in, please?'

Silence.

Suddenly Annie heard – quite clearly – a laugh!

She lunged against the door, but it was no good. Someone, James probably, was holding it shut. Annie frowned. She knew what she had to do. She would have to bide her time.

It was just a question of getting the timing right . . .

Chapter Two

Annie got the timing right.

She left it about fifteen minutes, crept up to the door, turned the handle – and burst in!

The boys jumped.

James hid something under his pillow.

Will look startled.

And Arthur just stared at her with his pale eyes.

'What are you doing?' said Annie.

'Nothing!' said James.

She looked hard at her brothers.

Then she looked at Arthur.

'Do tell me!' she pleaded.

'Nokun-doo!' said Arthur.

'What?' she said, puzzled.

'No . . . can . . . do,' said Arthur slowly, as if he was talking to someone very stupid.

'Can not do,' said Will.

'It just means we can't,' said James.

Arthur was smiling in a most annoying way. 'It's . . . well, it's rather a top-level thing, you see,' he said. 'We need to keep it under wraps.'

Annie could hardly believe her ears.

A top-level thing? Keep it under wraps?

But she was by far the best at
keeping secrets in the whole family!

How *dare* he?

Annie saw red. She leapt.

Not for Arthur, tempting though it was.

She leapt for the pillow – and
whatever it was James had hidden there.

But they were too quick for her.

Will grabbed her shirt, and James
grabbed her by
the wrist.

'Okay, chaps!' said Arthur. 'Do your stuff.'

They did 'their stuff'. Which meant bundling Annie out of the room . . .

'You're mean!' she shouted, as the door closed. 'Mean, mean, mean!'

She stood outside, blinking away her tears.

How dare the boys treat her like this!

She was as good as them any day!

And to think she had looked
forward to Arthur coming. She'd
even helped blow up his bed.
Arthur's drawly voice still
rang in her head. *A
top-level thing!* And
calling her brothers
chaps. Arthur Vance!
(Arthur *Pants*, more like!)
She stamped down to the
kitchen, where Mum was
changing the plug on
the toaster.

Annie poured out her woes.

'Oh, dear,' said Mum.

'Oh, dear?' cried Annie. 'Is that all
you have to say? Oh, dear?!'

'Well, what do you want me to do?'
Mum peered into her tool-box. 'Bang

their heads together and *make* them
play with you?'

'Hmm . . .' Annie quite liked the idea
of the head-banging.

'Forget it!' Mum held up a fuse.
'Thirteen amps, I think.'

'It's all Arthur! He's behind this. And
it's not fair!'

'Look, Annie,' said Mum. 'Sometimes people don't let you join in. It's something that happens in life.' She clicked the fuse into place. 'Just pretend you don't care – that's the best way.'

'Huh!' said Annie, and she stamped back to her room.

Well, Mum was no good.

Something that happened in life! What sort of attitude was *that*? Mums were supposed to *make* life fair, weren't they?

She slammed the door, and bounced crossly onto her bed. She bounced so hard that Greenfly, her old teddy, fell

off. She picked him up, and propped
him up on her pillow.

'Listen, Greenfly!' she said.

Greenfly looked back, unblinking.

'I'm going to find out the boys'
secret.'

Greenfly said nothing.

'You bet your black button eyes!'

Chapter Three

So Annie started her career as a spy. Project: find out the boys' secret! These were the things she thought of.

1. *Looking through the keyhole.* This was no good, for a very simple reason. James's door didn't have a keyhole.

2. *Listening with a glass to the wall.* This was a failure too. Which ever way Annie held the glass, she couldn't hear a thing.

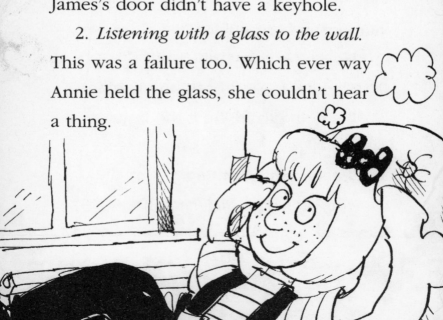

3. *A complicated plan to climb into the attic and drill a hole through James's ceiling*. A problem here. If Mum found out, she would – in James's words – 'go ballistic'. This meant, very, very, very cross. Having fallen out with three people in the house, Annie decided not to risk a ballistic Mum.

4. *Violence*. Perhaps she could kidnap the youngest member of the gang – Will – and *torture* (well, sit on) him until he told her the secret? Annie

rejected this idea too, mainly on 'ballistic
Mum' grounds.

So none of the above.

Annie would have to think again. She
sat Greenfly on her lap, and twirled his
arms round. Somehow that always
helped her think.

Pity James's door had no keyhole. Or
was it.

No keyhole meant . . . *no lock.*

It was about six when Mum stuck her

head round the door. 'Ah, Annie. Come down and choose what you want on your pizza.'

'Yum!' So Mum was making home-made pizza. That was one good thing about having a guest. The food got better.

Annie thought quickly. 'Just do me a surprise one!'

'Okay.' Mum went off to James's room.

A few minutes later she heard the boys walk past her room to the stairs. They were talking loudly about football. Annie wasn't fooled for a second. This was clearly to put her off the track. Whatever the secret was, it was certainly nothing to do with football. She just *knew* Arthur Pants wasn't interested in football.

She heard them go into the kitchen. Then Annie the Spy went into action. She crept along the corridor, opened the door into

James's room, and closed it softly
behind her.

The Spy looked round.

There was James's bed. There was James's chest of drawers. There was Arthur's blow-up bed by the wall (wouldn't she love to prick it with a pin–*pfffft!*). There was Arthur's big blue suitcase. And there was the desk with Dad's old computer on it.

Right, she thought, narrowing her eyes. Let's get cracking!

There was nothing under James's pillow – well, she hadn't really expected that. Or under his bed. Or in his cupboard. She couldn't quite bring herself to rummage through Arthur's suitcase (and, anyway, she was pretty sure it was locked). But finally she struck lucky. She felt towards the back of James's sock drawer, and a sock . . . crackled.

'Aha!' Annie thought of the detective
stories she had read.

She took it out, put a hand inside,
and pulled out an envelope.

Inside the envelope were three

home-made badges with some letters written on them. 'AJWUSS'. Annie stared. AJWUSS? AJWUSS? It didn't mean a thing. There was also a folded piece of paper. She unfolded it to find a picture of . . . well, what? It was a strange chart, with a lot of funny shapes on it. They were called things like 'Triangle' or 'Cigar' or 'Flat disc'. What could it all mean?

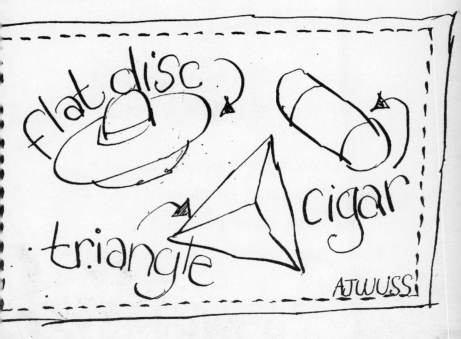

After puzzling a bit, Annie gave up. She put the things back in the envelope, the envelope back in the sock, and the sock back in the sock drawer. A good spy, she knew, leaves no traces . . .

She should have left the room then.

She should have, but she didn't.

She was burning to find out more. What was AJWUSS? What did those strange shapes mean? Were they anything to do with the boys' secret at all?

So she switched on the computer. Maybe she would find a clue there.

The computer moaned a bit, and finally a screen appeared. But bang in the middle appeared a panel. 'Please key in your password!' it said. *Drat*!

Annie scowled, and at that very moment she heard a noise.

She turned to see someone standing over her.

It was Arthur. 'Hold it right there!' he cried. Behind him stood James and Will.

Annie had been caught. Caught red-handed. And what did she do?

She *lied* (which is the sort of thing that happens when you start spying). 'Hello, chaps!' she said. 'I'm just checking your fuse!'

Chapter Four

The boys chucked her out again.

And they found a way of tilting a chair against the door to *keep* her out.

Still, Annie thought, at least she had found out something. She went to find Mum.

Mum was in the garage, looking out things for the seaside (the family were going later in the month).

'I can't find the puncture kit,' she said to Annie. 'Can you look on those shelves?'

There was all sorts of stuff on the garage shelves – tools, funnels, spray paint, an old sink plunger. But Annie couldn't see the puncture kit.

'Mum,' she said as she was looking. 'What's AJWUSS?'

'*What*?' said Mum.

'AJWUSS,' repeated Annie.

'Spell it.' Mum pulled some snorkelling flippers out of a bag.

Annie spelled it.

'You can have these flippers now.

They'll be too small for James.'

'But, Mum . . .' said Annie.

'Yes!' said Mum suddenly.

'Yes, you know what AJWUSS means?' said Annie eagerly.

'Yes, I've found the puncture kit!' Mum waved it above her head. Then she frowned. 'Now all I need is Dad's binoculars. I'm worried about them. I can't find them anywhere.'

'But what about AJWUSS?' said Annie.

'Haven't a clue!' said Mum.

*Cigar . . .
triangle . . . flat
disc . . .*

Annie and
Greenfly were
sitting at Annie's
window.

They were
watching the
boys in the garden. Or rather they were
watching the bushes in which the boys
were hiding.

*Cigar . . . triangle . . . flat
disc . . .*

The strange chart
of shapes
lingered

in Annie's mind. She puzzled and puzzled. Could the boys be making a modern sculpture? Er, no. Annie knew her brothers. Artists they were not.

The boys had lurked behind the bushes most of the afternoon. Annie saw most of Will, who seemed to be running a lot of errands. Once, red-faced, he hauled out Arthur's big blue suitcase. And several times he went to the kitchen for snacks. Snacks were something that Arthur Pants took seriously.

Cigar . . . triangle . . . flat disc . . . Annie racked her brains. A geometry project? *Not* likely.

Once she had gone down to the garden and started kicking a football around.

Will, on his way to the house, had looked over longingly. But a pink face had suddenly appeared in the bushes and hissed something. And Will had nodded, and gone on into the kitchen.

Cigar . . . triangle . . . flat disc . . .

'Annie?' Mum was calling up the stairs. 'Dad's on the phone from Germany.'

'Yup! Yip! Yippee!' Annie galloped downstairs.

'Don't tell him we've lost his binoculars,' said Mum, as she handed over the receiver.

'How are you, Annie-kins?' said Dad.

'I'm fine!' she said. 'But I'm a bit cross!'

'Oh? Why are you a bit cross?'

'Because of the boys!'

'What have the boys done?'

Annie drew a deep breath. 'They've got a secret, and they won't let me join

in, and they whisper and throw me out
of their room!'

'Goodness!' said Dad.

'It's all because of Arthur. It's since
he came.'

'Oh? So what's Arthur like?' said Dad.

'He's fat and he's got a pink face and
he makes Will run errands for him.'

'Sounds a charmer,' said Dad.

'He's not a charmer!' cried Annie.

'That was a joke,' said Dad.

'It's no joking matter, Dad,' said
Annie sternly.

'Sorry,' said Dad.

'Arthur Vance!' Annie said crossly.
'Arthur Pants is what I call him!'

Dad laughed. 'I hope not to his face.'

'No. To myself. And to Greenfly. He's
the only one on my side.' She paused.
'He doesn't make much of a gang, though.'

'Oh, I don't know,' said Dad. 'I
reckon you and Greenfly should be a
match for those boys, if you put your
mind to it.'

'Hmmm,' said Annie doubtfully.
Suddenly she had a thought. 'Dad?'

'Yes?'

'If I said cigar-shape and triangle and
flat disc, would it mean anything to you?'

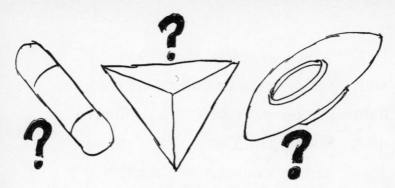

'Um . . . yes,' said Dad. 'It would. But I have to go. My boss is ringing through on the other line.'

'What would it mean to you?' said Annie.

'Oofos,' said Dad. 'Goodnight, Annie, sweet.' And he rang off.

Annie put down the phone slowly.

She didn't feel much better off. What on earth were *Oofos*?

Did you eat Oofos? Wear Oofos? Play with Oofos? Listen to Oofos? Or just put them in someone's bed to give them a nasty shock?

'Hmm,' said Mum, when Annie asked. 'I reckon he means UFOs.'

'Eh?' said Annie.

'Unidentified Flying Objects.'

'Eh?' said Annie.

'Flying Saucers.'

Chapter Five

Annie biked into the bushes. 'I know your secret!' she called as she crashed over.

The boys came out and stood around her.

'What is it, then?' said Arthur.

'UFOs!' said Annie, picking a twig out of her hair. 'Unidentified Flying Objects. And you've pinched Dad's binoculars to try and spot them!'

The boys looked at each other.

Annie drew a breath. 'I'd like to join

in!' she said. 'I'd be a help. Honestly. I've got the best eyes in the family, and I know lots of alien jokes.'

There was a silence.

Then Arthur spoke. 'You don't quite understand. This is serious. It isn't for kids.'

Annie gasped. 'Kids! Will is two years younger than me!'

'Nineteen months,' said Will.

'Anyway,' said James, 'it could be dangerous. We –'

'Ssssh!' said Arthur.

All three boys fell silent. And stayed silent.

There was nothing for it. Annie picked up her bike, and wheeled it away.

But she heard Will say, 'It's quite true – she *has* got the best eyes in the family.'

That evening Annie crept into Will's
room when the boys were in the
bathroom. There was a big book on his
bed. On the cover was . . . a strange
creature in a strange landscape. Annie
picked it up. It was a book about alien
monsters. Slowly she flicked through the
pages.

Urrgh! They were terrible-looking.
They chilled the blood. There was one
like an enormous spider. There was a
dinosaur-type with something red

dripping from its jaws. A cat-like
creature looked really quite friendly. But
the next picture was *scary*! It was like a
man – but not a man you would want
to be alone with. One bit. And he had a
laser-gun.

Suddenly she heard a noise behind
her.

She knew at once what it was. A
horrible alien monster.

Annie spun round.

It wasn't a horrible alien monster.

It was Will. His hair was wet.

'Will!' she gasped. 'It's you!'

He nodded. He didn't seem at all cross to find her there, reading the book.

'Annie?' said Will, sitting on the bed.

She looked at him. 'Yes?'

'I just . . . well, I just wanted to talk to you.'

'Okay. Go ahead.'

Will drew a breath. 'Arthur says . . . well, that aliens might be coming.'

'*What?*'

Will looked unhappy. 'You see, he's got all this radio equipment and a real proper

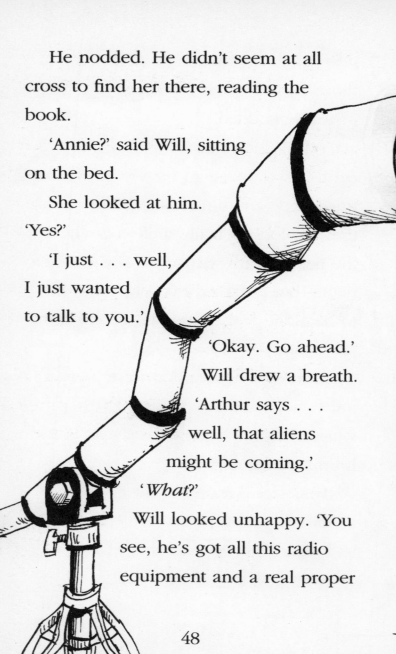

48

telescope.' He paused. 'That was the thing we hid when you came in.'

Annie nodded.

'Well, Arthur believes he's made contact with these aliens – I even heard the beeps. And he seems to think they're coming. Tonight.'

'*Tonight*?' She gaped at him.

Will nodded. 'At 20 hours.'

'Um . . . er . . .'

'Eight o'clock.'

There was silence.

Then Will spoke. 'I wish you were with us, Annie,' he said unhappily. 'But Arthur's –' He broke off.

'Yes,' said Annie. 'Arthur *is.*'

Chapter Six

It was 7.40 pm.

And suddenly Annie was frightened.

She was frightened for her brothers.

All right, she was a bit cross with the boys. But she still didn't want them to be . . . *dissolved* or something by aliens. She didn't even want Arthur Pants to be dissolved by aliens.

She thought about the book of aliens. The giant spider. The dinosaur with something bloody hanging from its jaws.

That horrible man. Aargh! Even if he didn't get out of the space-ship, he could probably laser them. Aaargh! Aaargh!

She went to find Mum.

Mum was upstairs, sorting a pile of laundry. 'Now, what will the boys wear tomorrow . . .?'

'Maybe they won't need anything tomorrow,' said Annie in a small voice.

'Well, they can't go on wearing today's things!' said Mum. 'They're filthy!'

'Mum?' said Annie.

Mum took a red sock from the pile of clothes. 'Mmmm?'

'Mum, there may be aliens coming tonight.'

Mum didn't scream or faint or anything. She said, 'Good heavens!'

'I'm worried, Mum!' said Annie. 'I don't want them to dissolve the boys.'

'I should hope not!' said Mum.

'But, Mum!' wailed Annie. 'You're not taking this seriously. There may be some aliens from outer space coming! They could

laser them or dissolve them or beam them up or anything!'

'Now, Annie,' said Mum. 'You're letting these games run away with you.' She picked out another red sock. 'I don't think any aliens are coming.'

'But if they are?' said Annie in a whisper.

'If they are, there's not much we can do about it.' Mum bundled the red socks together. 'Except ring the Ministry of Defence.' She laughed. 'And a fat lot *they*'d do about it!'

Chapter Seven

So Mum was no good, thought Annie grimly.

She wasn't going to help.

It was up to her!

And suddenly she had an idea.

Annie looked at her watch. *Quarter to eight*. She had just fifteen minutes. She would have to be quick.

She ran downstairs. Were the boys already in the garden? Her plan wouldn't work if they were. No, she could hear James and Will talking by the back door. She was in time!

Quickly Annie unlocked the cellar door, and turned the cellar lights on.

Then she called out. 'James! Will!'

They came back into the kitchen, looking impatient. James had his camera strung round his neck. Will was wearing Dad's binoculars.

'What is it?' James glanced at his watch.

Annie nodded to the cellar door. 'Arthur's down there.'

'In the cellar?' said James. 'He was in the garden a second ago.'

'No, he's down there,' said Annie. 'He needs some help bringing something up.'

James scowled. 'Well, he's left it very –' But he started walking down the cellar stairs. As soon as Will followed him, Annie gently closed the cellar door, and put the latch on. First there was silence. Then someone pushed the door. And soon both boys were banging and shouting.

They were angry. Very angry. But safe. Very safe . . .

Some time later, having glanced in the
garden, Annie unlatched the cellar door.

Two furious brothers emerged.

Then Arthur came in from the
garden.

He was completely un-lasered.
Totally undissolved. In fact he looked
even more solid than usual.

They all gazed at him.

'Did . . . did you see anything?' said
Will.

'Well, yes . . .' Arthur looked rather pleased with himself. 'In fact I did.'

'What?' cried James. 'What did you see?'

'Well . . .' said Arthur, a fat smile on his face. 'I saw this shape hovering over the garden. With . . . with some lights in it.'

'Wow!' said James.

Will just looked at him open-mouthed.

'So there really was something . . .' breathed

58

James. He looked accusingly at Annie.
'And we'd have seen it too. If it hadn't
been for *her*.'

Arthur nodded. 'But perhaps it was a
good thing,' he said. 'You have to be
pretty brave to see that sort of thing.' He
smirked. 'It's no good if you run
shrieking at the first sign of something
strange.'

Annie met his eye – and her stomach
turned over.

Chapter Eight

Annie sat on the bed, her mind racing.

Greenfly sat on the bed, his arm racing.

For Annie was twirling Greenfly's arm round . . .

She saw it all now. Arthur hadn't seen any weird object. He hadn't seen any UFO. *Of course* he hadn't. And he

had made all that up about the radio
contact with aliens.

He was a hoaxer. A simple hoaxer.
And she had played into his hands by
locking up her brothers. After that he
could pretend he really *had*
seen something. And now
Arthur was *crowing* – saying
he was braver than them.
Fat pink-faced Arthur Pants
braver than her brothers?
Braver than her James and
Will?

Annie wasn't going to put up with it. No way!

Greenfly was at his arm exercises for a long time that night. He even did some leg exercises.

At last Annie knew what her plan was.

She spent the whole of the next morning in the garage.

She hummed as she worked. 'Anything you can do, I can do better. I can do anything better than YOU!' And she jumped around in the flippers to get used to wearing them.

The sink plunger would *not* stay on. But she had better luck with one of the funnels.

She also had a quiet word with Will.

He wasn't a problem. He hadn't been *that* cross about the cellar (whatever he pretended). And he was getting a bit fed up waiting on James and Arthur.

She laughed when he told her the password to the computer. AJWUSS! Of course. The Arthur, James and Will UFO-Spotting Society. Why hadn't she thought of it before?

Chapter Nine

It is not easy, sitting in a bush with a funnel strapped to your head.

It is the sort of thing you only do if you are determined.

Annie was determined.

It was a still a bit wobbly, the funnel, but it was a good colour. Annie had sprayed it with silver paint. She had also sprayed her flippers and her belt with silver paint. They looked quite effective

against her black clothes. Her face
make-up had been left over from
Halloween. And the laser gun (made out
of Mum's broken hair-drier) was pretty
neat. The bit she was proudest of,

though, was the air vent tube from the old tumble-drier, which she had flung round her neck like a feather boa.

She had also been thinking about Special Effects.

She couldn't run to dry ice, but she had a nice big pot of talcum powder. She also had an old electric somersaulting bear, which made a good loud *whirr-boing* sound! She smiled to herself. Yes, she was *ready!*

Her watch said ten to nine. She was glad she had put 9 pm on the computer message. It would all be more effective in the dusk. She grinned. She was looking forward to her encounter with the members of the Arthur, James and Will UFO-Spotting Society. They were about to spot more than they had bargained for. Yes, indeed!

A few minutes later she heard voices. Then the voices came nearer.

The boys stopped about fifteen metres from the bushes.

'Where exactly did you see the shape come from last time?' James was saying.

'Um, well . . . sort of thereish,' Arthur
muttered. He didn't sound as confident
as usual.

'Amazing the way they fed that
message direct into our computer,' said
James. 'They didn't do that last time, did
they?'

'No!' said Arthur shortly.

'Do you think we'll see anything?'
Will said.

'Shouldn't think so,' said Arthur.

'Why not?' said James. '*You* did after
all.

Annie watched the three of them stare up into the sky.

'I keep wondering what "surface level contact" means,' said James. 'You know, in the message. Perhaps it means the ground. Maybe we shouldn't be looking for a space-ship at all. Maybe we should be looking down here. For aliens.'

'It's getting cold,' said Arthur. 'And your mother might be cross if she catches us. Perhaps we ought to go in.'

Now!

Blast-off!

Annie unlocked the catch on the somersaulting bear. *Whirr-boing! Whirr-boing!*

Then she took a handful of talcum powder, threw it high up in front of her – and flippered forward into the cloud. '*Fleeeeeeeeeeeeeep!*' she went. And she waved her laser gun.

There was a long second of silence.

And then Arthur gave one
terrible scream, and ran.

Will just stared at her, open-mouthed.
James looked at Arthur, running for
the house.

Then he looked back at
her. And then he did
something that Annie
would remember for
the rest of her life.

He started . . .
walking towards her.

Step by step he
drew closer.

Annie watched his
pale determined face –
and a strange feeling of pride washed
through her.

Suddenly he stopped a few metres
away. He narrowed his eyes at her, and
then, gradually, his face cleared.

'Annie!' he called softly. 'Annie! It's you, isn't it?'

There was silence.

And then Annie drew a breath. 'Yes.' She took the funnel off her head. 'It's me.'

For a second James just stood there. Then he threw back his head – and laughed. 'Annie! I should have guessed!'

He turned to Will, who had come up behind him. 'You knew all the time, did you?'

Will nodded shyly.

'Yes,' said Annie. 'I couldn't have him getting too frightened. You and Arthur were a different matter.' She grinned. 'Especially Arthur.'

They all looked towards the house.

'Poor old Arthur,' said James. 'You gave him a real fright!'

Annie smiled. 'Reckon I did.'

James shook his head slowly. 'Oh, Annie,' he said. 'Oh, Annie.'

There was silence. And then Annie said, 'James?'

'Yes?'

'Did you really think I might be an alien?'

James frowned. 'I know it sounds mad now, but Arthur got us all so worked up.' He shrugged. 'I suppose I did.'

'You really thought I might be an alien? And you still came up to me!' Annie felt her eyes fill with tears. 'Oh, James, how could you be so brave? And so *stupid*?!!'

Chapter Ten

'*Tea-parties?*' said James. 'You want us to play tea-parties?'

'Yes,' said Annie.

She hid a smile. She was only going to get her own way for a bit. She was going to make the most of it.

'I've never played tea-parties before,' said Will.

'Oh, it's quite easy!' said Annie. 'Come on, I've got it all ready.'

She led them out to the old wooden box, where she had laid the tea. Greenfly was already sitting at his place. 'You sit there, James,' she said, pointing to the end. 'And I thought here for Will.' She patted a place. 'And over there by the tea-pot is for Arthur.' She smiled at him. 'I thought you could do the tea, Arthur.'

Arthur seemed too dazed to object.
'Um . . . all right.'

They sat down.

'Tea-time, all!' said Annie gaily. She looked round at her little party – she was really enjoying herself.

No one met her eye.

'Arthur?' said Annie in an encouraging tone.

And Arthur picked up the tea-pot.